ROBERT LOUIS STEVENSON

THE
BOTTLE
IMP

The vocabulary is based on
Michael West: A General Service List of
English Words, revised & enlarged edition 1953
Pacemaker Core Vocabulary, 1975
Salling/Hvid: English-Danish Basic Dictionary, 1970
J. A. van Ek: The Threshold Level for Modern Language
Learning in Schools, 1976

EDITORS
Aage Salling *Denmark*
Erik Hvid *Denmark*
Revised edition by Robert Dewsnap, 1980

Illustrations: Oskar Jørgensen

Printed in Denmark by
Sangill Bogtryk & offset, Holme Olstrup

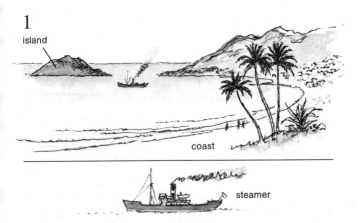

1

island

coast

steamer

There was a man in the *island* of Hawaii. I shall call him Keawe. He is still living, and no-one must know his name. This man was poor, but he could read and write like a teacher. He worked for some time on the island *steamers,* and then on a boat on the *coast*. At last Keawe decided to see the great world and big cities; so he went to San Francisco.

This is a fine town. Many of the people there have a lot of money. Some of them live on a hill in fine houses. One day Keawe was walking on this hill with his *pocket* full of money.

"What fine houses these are!" he was thinking.

pocket

"And how happy those people must be who live in them!"

He was thinking of this, and then he came to a house that was smaller than the others. But it was as fine as a *flower,* and the windows gave off light like *diamonds.* Keawe stopped to look at it.

So stopping, he saw a man that looked out of a window. Keawe could see him as clearly as you can see a fish in the water.

The man smiled and smiled as if to tell Keawe to come in; and he met him at the door of the house.

"My house is a fine house, isn't it?" he said. "Please come and look at the rooms."

So he took Keawe all over the house. And everything in it was as good as good can be.

"This is a beautiful house," Keawe said. "If I lived in it, I should be laughing all day. How is it, then, that you are not?"

"If you like," the man said, "you can have one like it. Or even finer. You have some money, I think?"

"I have fifty dollars," Keawe said. "But a house like this will cost more than fifty dollars."

flower

diamond

4

"I am sorry that you have no more," the man said. "But you shall have it for fifty dollars."

"The house?" Keawe asked.

"No, not the house," the man said, "but the bottle. For I must tell you one thing. This house, and the garden, and all the things I have, came out of a small bottle. Here it is!"

And he took out a small round bottle with a long *neck*. The glass was white, and in it something moved. But what it was, you could not see.

"This is the bottle," the man said.

Keawe laughed. "This is a thing I don't understand."

"It came from *hell*," the man said, "and an *imp* lives in it. Look! You can see it moving. If a man buys this bottle, the imp will do everything for him. All that he wants – a house like this, or even a city, or money – all this can be his. He only has to say the word. Napoleon had this bottle. But he sold it, and fell."

"And yet you want to sell it?" Keawe asked.

"I have all I want," said the man, "and I am getting old. There is one thing the imp cannot do. He cannot make life longer. Also, if a man

---

neck, see page 15
hell, the place where bad people go when they die
imp, see page 15

has the bottle when he dies, he goes to hell."

"Well!" said Keawe. "I am certainly not going to buy such a thing."

"Listen," the man answered. "You only have to get what you want. Then you sell the bottle again."

"Well," Keawe said. "I see two things: you are not happy, and you sell this bottle very *cheap.*"

"I am getting old," the man said. "Like you, I do not want to die and go to hell. But I must tell you one thing. When *the devil* brought the bottle into the world, it cost a lot of money, many million dollars.

"But you must sell it cheaper than you bought it. The price has fallen all the time, and the bottle is now very cheap. I paid only ninety dollars. And I must sell it cheaper – or it will come back to me."

"How do I know that all this is true?" Keawe asked.

"Try it," the man said. "Give me your fifty dollars, take the bottle, and *wish* your fifty dollars back into your pocket. If you don't

---

cheap, for little money
the devil, the lord of hell
wish, shut your eyes and ask for something

get them, I will take the bottle back."

"Well, I will do that," Keawe said. And he gave the man his money, and the man handed him the bottle.

"Imp of the bottle," Keawe said, "I want my fifty dollars back." And there was the money in his pocket.

"Now good morning," said the man, "and the devil go with you!"

"Stop," Keawe said, "here, take your bottle back."

"You have bought it cheaper than I," the man said. "Now it is yours." And with these words he called his Chinese boy, who showed Keawe out of the house.

Now, when Keawe was in the street with the bottle under his arm, he began to think. First he looked at his money. It was there all right.

"This seems true," Keawe said. "Now let us try something else."

It was twelve o'clock, but there were not many people in the street. Keawe put the bottle on the ground and walked away. He looked back, and there was the bottle in the same place. He looked back again, and the bottle was still there. A third time he looked back, and there was the bottle in his pocket with the long neck showing.

"This seems to be true, too," Keawe said.

Next, he bought a *corkscrew* in a shop, and went out into the fields. There he tried to pull the *cork* out. But every time he put the screw in, out it came again.

"This is some new sort of cork," he said, and the *sweat* began to run down his face.

On his way back to his ship he saw a shop, where they sold all sorts of things. There he had a good idea. He went in and asked the man to buy the bottle for one hundred dollars. The man laughed, and said that he would give him five. Then they talked for half an hour. In the end, the man gave Keawe sixty dollars and set the bottle in his window.

"Now," Keawe said. "I have sold for sixty what I bought for fifty. Soon I shall know if the other thing is true."

So he went back to his ship.

When he opened his *chest,* there was the bottle; and it had come more quickly than himself.

corkscrew

cork

---

sweat, water coming out of your skin when you are hot
chest, see page 10

chest

Questions

1. Why does Keawe go to San Francisco?
2. Why does Keawe stop outside the house?
3. What does the man want to sell to Keawe?
4. What is in the bottle?
5. Why does he want to sell it?
6. Why is the bottle so cheap?
7. What does Keawe do in the field?
8. Why does the bottle not stay with the man in the shop?
9. Where does Keawe find the bottle when he comes back to the ship?

2

Now Keawe had a friend named Lopaka.

"What is the matter?" asked Lopaka.

They were alone in their room, and Keawe told him all.

"I don't understand this," Lopaka said. "You have the bottle; it can give you good things, so why not use it? Then, if it is all as you wish, I will buy the bottle myself."

"My idea," Keawe said, "is to have a beautiful house and garden. On the coast, where I *was born*. There will be sun coming in at the window, flowers in the garden, glass in the windows, pictures on the walls. Just like the house I was in this morning. Only one floor higher, and with *balconies* like the King's house. There I shall live with my friends and family."

"Well," said Lopaka, "let us carry the bottle

schooner

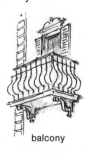

balcony

---

was born, started life

back to Hawaii. If all comes true, I will buy the bottle and wish for a *schooner*."

Soon the ship came back to Honolulu, with Keawe and Lopaka and the bottle. When they left the ship, they met a friend. He told them that Keawe's *uncle* was dead. Keawe began to cry. But Lopaka was thinking to himself, and after some time he said to Keawe:

"I have been thinking. Hadn't your uncle lands in Hawaii?"

"Yes," said Keawe, "at Hookena."

"And these lands will now be yours?" Lopaka asked.

"Yes, they will!" said Keawe, and began to cry.

"No," said Lopaka, "don't cry. I have been thinking: this is just the place for your house. Perhaps it came from the bottle."

"If this is so," said Keawe, "it is a very bad way to help me. It kills my family. But I **was** thinking of such a place."

"The house is not built yet," Lopaka said.

"And it will not be," Keawe said, "for my uncle had no money."

"Let us go to the *lawyer*," Lopaka said. "I still

---

schooner, see page 11
uncle, the brother of his father or mother
lawyer, one who takes care of land and money for people

have this idea in my mind."

So they came to the lawyer's. There they found that Keawe's uncle had become very rich in the end; and there was much money.

"And here is the money for the house," said Lopaka.

"If you are thinking of a new house," said the lawyer, "I know a very good *architect*."

"Better and better," said Lopaka. "Let us go."

So they went to the architect, and he had *drawings* on his table.

"You want something good?" he said. "How do you like this?" and he handed Keawe a drawing.

Now when Keawe saw the drawing, he cried out; for it was the picture of the house of his *dreams*.

drawing

architect, one who makes drawings for houses
dreams, what he sees when he closes his eyes

So he told the architect all that he wanted. Then he asked him what the house would cost. The architect asked many questions. Then he told Keawe what the house would cost. And that was as much money as Keawe had.

Keawe and Lopaka looked at each other.

"I can see," Keawe said, "that I am to have this house. It comes from the devil, and that is not good. I will make no more wishes as long as I live."

So they left the architect, and Keawe and Lopaka took ship again, to Australia. And all the time Keawe took care to make no more wishes. When they got back the house was ready, and they went to see it.

Now, the house stood on a mountain-side with a garden round it with all sorts of flowers and *fruit*-trees. It was three floors high, with great rooms and balconies on all sides. The windows were of glass, there were tables and chairs, and pictures of beautiful women, and of men fighting, books with many pictures, clocks, and *musical-boxes*. And from the balconies

musical-box

---

fruit: a banana is a fruit

Keawe could see the sea and all the ships going up to Hookena.

"Well," said Lopaka, "is it all just as you wished?"

"Words cannot say it," answered Keawe. "It is better than I dreamed."

"This may not come from the bottle at all," Lopaka said. "So if I buy the bottle and I do not get the schooner, what then? I don't want to put my hand into the fire for nothing. So before I buy the bottle, let me see the imp; after that, here is the money."

"There is only one thing that I don't like," said Keawe. "The imp may not be very nice to

imp —

neck —

look at. You may not want to buy the bottle if you see him."

"I have given you my word," Lopaka said.

"So come and let us look at you, Mr Imp!"

At these words, the imp looked out of the bottle, and was in again. And there sat Keawe and Lopaka and could not speak or move. Night came before they could say a word. Then Lopaka gave Keawe the money and took the bottle.

Lopaka went down the mountain, and Keawe stood on the balcony. He asked *God* to take care of his friend; and he thanked him because the bottle was gone.

But the next day came, and the new house was so beautiful that Keawe forgot all about the bottle. One day followed another, and Keawe lived there, as happy as a man can be. He could not walk through the rooms without singing. And the people heard him. They told each other what they had seen and heard. And they called the house the Great House – or sometimes the Bright House, for Keawe had a Chinaman who kept the house clean and *bright*.

God, the father who made the world
bright, light and clear

Questions

1. What is Keawe's house to be like?

2. What does the lawyer tell Keawe?

3. What does the architect show him?

4. Where does Keawe go while they are building the house?

5. What is Keawe's house like?

6. What does Lopaka want before he buys the bottle?

7. Is Keawe happy in his new house?

8. Who keeps house for Keawe?

3

Time went by. Then one day Keawe went to see some friends, who lived at Kailua. There he had a good time. He left early the next morning, for he wanted to go back to his house.

As he was riding, he saw a woman swimming in the sea. When he came up to the place, she had put on her red *holoku*. And he saw that her eyes were bright and kind. And Keawe stopped his horse.

"I thought I knew everyone in this country," he said. "How is it that I don't know you?"

"I am Kokua, daughter of Kiano," said the girl, "and I have just come back from Oahu. Who are you?"

"I will tell you who I am," Keawe said. "Only not now. If you know who I am, you may not give me a true answer. But tell me first: are you married?"

Kokua only laughed. "It is you who ask questions," she said. "Are you married yourself?"

"I am not, Kokua," Keawe answered. "But I have met you at the roadside, and I saw your eyes, and I loved you at once. If you don't want to see me, say so, and I will go home. But if you like me just as well as any other young man, say so too. Then we will go to your father's house,

holoku

and I will talk to the good man in the morning."

Kokua didn't say a word, but she looked at the sea and laughed.

"Kokua," said Keawe, "if you say nothing, let us go to your father's house."

Now, when they came to the door, Kiano came out and called Keawe by name. At that, the girl looked at them, for she had heard of the Great House. The next day, Keawe had a word with Kiano, and later found the girl alone.

"Kokua," he said, "I did not want to tell you who I was, because I have so fine a house. I was afraid that you would think too much of the house; and too little of the man who loves you. If you want me to go away, say so."

"No," said Kokua, but this time she did not laugh. "Here is this young man," she thought. "I met him only yesterday. If I marry him, I must leave my father and mother and the place where I was born."

Keawe left her and rode up the hill to his house, singing all the way. And as he sat at table, he was still singing. The sun went down in the sea, and the Chinaman heard him sing between the mouthfuls.

"For the first time," said Keawe to himself, "I will use my fine bath with the hot and cold water."

So the Chinaman got the bath ready. He heard Keawe sing – and then stop.

He listened. Then he called to Keawe to ask if all was well. Keawe answered "Yes," and told him to go to bed.

All night long the Chinaman heard him walking round and round the balconies.

Now, when Keawe took off his clothes, he saw on his body a small *spot*. And it was then

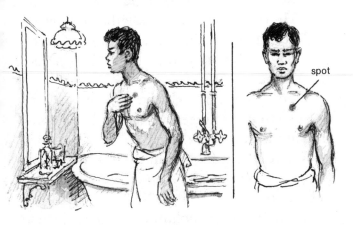

that he stopped singing. For he knew that spot, and knew that he had got the *Chinese Evil*.

Now, it is a bad thing for any man to get the Chinese Evil. And to have to leave a house so

---

Chinese Evil, a bad spot from China. If Keawe touches other people, they will have the spot too

beautiful, and go away from all his friends to the north coast of Molokai. And what did it mean to a man like Keawe, who had met his love only that morning?

"I can go to Molokai," Keawe said to himself. "There, I can live with the other people who have got the Chinese Evil. What have I done wrong? Why must I meet Kokua this morning, and then have to go away from her tomorrow?"

Now, you can see what kind of man Keawe was. He could perhaps live with the Chinese Evil for many years, and perhaps nobody would see it. But how could he do that and not tell Kokua?

A little after midnight he remembered the bottle. He remembered the day when he saw the imp look out of the bottle.

"What!" he said. "Would I buy the bottle once only to get a house, and not do it again to get Kokua?"

"I must go to Honolulu first," he said, "and find Lopaka. Now I have only one hope: to find the bottle I was so glad to sell."

Questions

1. What does Keawe see on his way home?

2. What does he ask the girl?

3. Who is she?

4. What does she ask him?

5. Why doesn't Keawe tell her who he is?

6. Why does Keawe want to use his bathroom for the first time?

7. Why does he stop singing?

8. Why does he want to buy the bottle back?

4

The next morning he sent a letter to Kiano. Then he rode down the hill to the steamer. It was raining, and his horse went very slowly. He remembered how fast he had ridden up the hill the day before, and was *sad*. He came down to Hookena. There were all the people to meet the steamer. They were all talking and laughing. Only Keawe sat there looking at the rain and did not say a word.

"Keawe of the Great House is sad," said one to another, and so he was.

Sitting on the *deck* of the steamer he looked at

deck

the house of Kiano a long way off over the sea.

There it was, and there by the door was the red holoku.

---

sad, not happy
queen, the wife of a king

"Oh, *queen* of my heart," he said, "I will do anything to win you."

Keawe walked the deck all night. The next day when they passed Molokai, he was still walking up and down like an animal in a *zoo*.

Once in Honolulu, Keawe stepped out among the people and began to ask for Lopaka. It seemed that he had got a schooner, and had gone fishing among the islands. Keawe remembered a friend of Lopaka's, a lawyer in the town (I must not tell you his name), and asked where this man lived. They said that he had grown very rich, and had a fine new house at Waikiki, and this gave Keawe an idea. He went to the lawyer's house.

"You are a friend of Lopaka's," said Keawe, "and Lopaka bought something from me. Perhaps you can help me to find it."

"Mr Keawe," said the lawyer, "I do not like to speak about this, but I think I can help you."

And he named the name of a man, which again I shall not tell you. So it was for days. Keawe went from one to another. They all had fine clothes and new houses. But when he said what he wanted, their faces became dark. "When I see a white face and I hear crying,"

---

zoo, a garden for strange animals

Keawe said, "I shall know I am near the bottle."

At last he was told to go to a young white man in Beritania Street.

When he came to the place, it was of course a very fine new house.

Keawe went up to the door. A young man came out, white in the face and black about the eyes. "Here it is, to be sure," thought Keawe. So he said, "I have come to buy the bottle."

"The bottle," the young man repeated, "to buy the bottle?"

"Yes," Keawe said, "I have come to buy the bottle. *What is the price* now?"

"The price! You don't know the price?"

"That is what I am asking you," Keawe said. "Is there anything wrong with the price?"

"It has dropped very low since your time, Mr Keawe," said the young man.

"Well, well, what did you pay for it?"

"Two cents," he said.

"What?" said Keawe. "Then you can sell it only for one cent. And he who buys it – – – –."

The young man fell down in front of Keawe. "Buy it," he said. "Oh, why did I ever buy it! I had taken some money in the shop where I work; and I didn't know what to do."

---

what is the price? how much does it cost?

"Poor man," said Keawe. "Give me the bottle, and here is a five-cent piece."

The young man gave Keawe back four cents, and Keawe got the bottle.

As soon as Keawe had it in his hands, he wished the spot on his body away. And when he got back to his hotel and took off his clothes, his skin was as fine as a baby's.

But Keawe thought no more of the Chinese Evil, and little enough of Kokua; for he had only one thought, that now the bottle was his for ever and ever.

Away in front of him he saw only the fire of hell.

Questions

1. Where does Keawe go to get the bottle?
2. How will he know when he is near the bottle?
3. Who has the bottle?
4. What is the price of the bottle?
5. What does Keawe wish for when he has the bottle?
6. Why does Keawe almost forget Kokua?

5

In the evening, Keawe felt a little better and remembered something. It was the night when the *band* played at the hotel. There he went, because he did not like to be alone; and there, among happy people, he walked up and down; and all the time he saw before him the red fire of hell. After two hours he heard the band play Hiki-ao-ao; that was the song he had sung with Kokua, and he felt strong again.

"It is done now," he said; "let me take the good with the bad."

And he went back to Hawaii by the first steamer. As soon as possible, he was married to Kokua, and carried her up the hill to the Bright House.

Now, when these two were together, Keawe's heart was still; but as soon as he was alone he saw the red fire of hell before him.

The girl was so beautiful that it pleased everybody to see her. She was always singing, and went up and down in the Bright House, the brightest thing in it.

But there came a day when her feet began to be heavy, and she stopped singing. Each of them sat on his or her own balcony. One day, Keawe heard someone crying. He found Kokua

band

on the floor, her face wet with *tears*.

"You do well to cry in this house," he said. "And yet I would give the head off my body to make you happy."

"Happy!" she cried. "Keawe, when you lived alone in your Bright House, you were a happy man. That is what everybody said. Then you married poor Kokua. What is wrong with her? From that day you have not smiled. I thought I was pretty; and I knew that I loved you."

"Poor Kokua," said Keawe. He sat down by her side, and tried to take her hand, but she took it away.

"Poor Kokua – my beautiful wife. I thought I could not tell you all. But now I shall do so. Then you will understand how much I loved you. And how much I love you still; so that I can smile when I see you."

---

tears, water from her eyes

32

Then he told her all, even from the beginning.

"You have done all this for me?" she cried. "Then what do I care?" and she cried and put her arms around his neck.

"Ah, child," said Keawe. "When I think of the fires of hell, I care very much."

"A man cannot be lost because he loved Kokua," she said. "I tell you, Keawe, I shall save you with my own hands."

"Ah, my dear," he cried. "You could die a hundred times; but I should still be alone to go to hell."

"You know nothing," she said. "I went to school in Honolulu. I tell you I shall save you. What is this you are saying about a cent? There is France; there, they have a *coin* which they call

coins

a centime. Centimes go five to the cent. We could not do better. Come, Keawe, let us go to the French islands. Let us go to Tahiti as fast as a ship can carry us. There we have four centimes, three centimes, two centimes, one centime; the bottle can be sold four times yet. Come, Keawe, pur your arms round me and let us go."

Early the next morning she took Keawe's old chest. First she put the bottle in, and then all their best clothes and the finest things in the house. "For," she said, "we must look like rich people; if not, who will believe in the bottle?"

They told people that they were going to the United States. From Honolulu they went to San Francisco. But from there they took a steamer to Papeete, the biggest place in the French islands of Tahiti.

They thought it best to take a house, to show people that they had money enough. This was very easy so long as they had the bottle. Kokua asked the imp for twenty or a hundred dollars when she wanted money.

They got on well with the people after some time, and learnt to speak French. But when they began to speak about the bottle, people stayed away from them. Some did not believe what they said. To get everything they wanted for four centimes? What an idea! They just laughed. And the last man who bought the bottle would go to hell. That made people's faces grow dark.

Sometimes Keawe and Kokua sat at night in their new house and did not say a word. Other times, they had the bottle out on the floor and sat all evening and looked at it.

At such times they did not like to go to bed. Even if they did, one of them got up and left the house to walk under the trees in the little garden or along the sea in the moonlight.

Questions

1. What does Keawe do when he comes home?

2. Why does Kokua stop singing?

3. What does Keawe tell her?

4. What does Kokua want to do to save Keawe?

5. Where do they go?

6. Where do people think they have gone?

7. How do they live in Tahiti?

8. Why do they live in a fine house?

9. Why do people stay away from them?

10. Why do they walk under the trees in the moonlight?

One night it was so when Kokua opened her eyes. Keawe was gone. She felt in his bed. It was cold. She sat up in bed.

The room was bright with moonlight, and she could hear the wind. She could also hear another sound. She got out of bed, and looked out. There under the trees lay Keawe, and he was crying.

Kokua wanted to run out and speak to him. But she went back into the house.

"Oh!" she thought. "Now at last I know what I must do."

She put on her clothes, took four centimes in her hand, and went out. The town was sleeping, but she heard somebody under the trees. It was an old man.

"Old man," she said, "what are you doing here in the cold night?"

The old man was not well, and he could hardly speak.

"Will you do something for me?" said Kokua. "Will you help a daughter of Hawaii?"

"So you are that woman from Hawaii. I have heard of you, and I will have nothing to do with you."

"Sit down here," said Kokua, "and let me tell

you a story." And she told the story of Keawe
from the beginning to the end. "And now," she
said, "will you go to Keawe and buy the bottle

for me? He will not sell it to me, but he will to you. Here are your four centimes."

"Give me the coins and wait for me here," said the old man.

Now, when Kokua stood alone in the street, she seemed to see the fires of hell before her. And she wanted to run away, but she could not.

The old man came back with the bottle in his hand. "I have done what you asked me," he said.

"Before you give it to me," said Kokua, "ask the imp to make you well again."

"I am an old man. I will not have the devil do anything for me. Take the bottle."

"All right," said Kokua at last. "There is your money."

Kokua put the bottle under her holoku, said goodbye to the old man, and went off. She did not know where she was going. Sometimes she walked, and sometimes she ran.

In the morning, she came back to the house, and found Keawe sleeping like a child.

"Now, Keawe," she thought. "Tomorrow you can sing and laugh again; but for Kokua there will be no more sleep, no more singing."

With that she lay down in the bed by his side and slept at once.

Later on, Keawe told her about the old man,

but she could not answer him. They had break-fast, but she did not eat a thing, only heard Keawe talk and laugh.

"He who has the bottle now," said Keawe, "will go to hell. Can't you see the fire – brrr."

"Oh, Keawe! I could not laugh if another man was going to hell instead of me."

Keawe felt that she was right, and grew angry.

"Do you think you are a good wife? Why can't you smile and laugh? If you thought of me at all, you would be a good, happy wife and go out with me."

With these words he went out, and Kokua was alone.

Keawe walked about the town all day. He met friends and drank with them. They went into the country together, and there drank more. And all the time Keawe was thinking of Kokua, and that made him drink even more.

Now, there was an old white man drinking with him. This was a bad man, who loved to drink and to see others drink too much. He made Keawe drink more and more. Soon there was no more money.

"Look here," he said, "you are rich, you have a bottle or something."

"Yes," said Keawe, "I will go back to my wife

and get some money. She keeps it."

"Never you give a woman money," said the man. "You look after her."

Back in town, Keawe asked the white man to wait for him. Then he went up to the house and looked in the back door. There was Kokua on the floor, and before her the bottle with its long neck.

For a long time, Keawe stood there and looked in at the door. Then he began to think – and understood.

He closed the door, went round the house, and then came in by the front door. He spoke to Kokua.

"I have been drinking all day," he said. "I have been with good friends, and have only come back for money."

"You do well to use your own," said Kokua.

"I do well in all things," said Keawe, and he went to the chest and took out some money. But he saw that there was no bottle in the chest. "It is as I thought," he said to himself. "She bought it."

"Oh," cried Kokua, "give me a kind word only."

"Let us always be good one to the other," said Keawe, and was gone out of the house.

Outside in the street, there was the old white man waiting.

"My wife has the bottle," said Keawe. "You must help me to get it, or there will be no more money tonight."

"Is it really true, what you say about the bottle?" asked the man.

"Look at my face and tell me if it is true."

"Yes, it is."

"Well, then, here are two centimes; you go to my wife and buy the bottle. Then I will buy it from you for one centime. But don't tell her that you come from me."

"Very well, I will try."

So the old man went up to the house, and Keawe stood waiting. It seemed to him that a long time passed. Then he heard the old man singing under the trees.

Keawe looked up, and saw the old man with the devil's bottle in his pocket, and a bottle of wine in his hand. And as Keawe looked at him, he drank.

"You have it," said Keawe. "I see that."

"Hands off!" cried the old man. "Take a step nearer me and I'll kill you."

"What do you mean?" cried Keawe.

"Mean?" cried the man. "This is a very good bottle, that's what I mean. How I got it for two centimes, I can't understand. But you certainly shan't have it for one."

"You mean that you won't sell it?" asked Keawe.

"No, sir!" cried the old man. "But I'll give you a drink of wine, if you like."

"Listen!" said Keawe. "The man who has that bottle goes to hell."

"I think I am going there in any case," said the man. "And this bottle is the best thing to take with me. No, sir! This is my bottle now, and you can go and find another. And if you won't have a drink, I'll have one myself. And good-night to you."

And the old man went down the road to the town, -- and there goes the bottle out of the story.

But Keawe ran to Kokua light as the wind, and very happy they were that night. And very happy they have been, ever since then, in the Bright House.

Questions

1. Where does Kokua see Keawe in the night?
2. What does she tell the old man about Keawe?
3. Why doesn't the old man want to use the bottle?
4. Why is Keawe happy the next morning?
5. What do you think: is Kokua a good wife?
6. What does Keawe do in the country?
7. Why does he come back for more money?
8. Does he find money at home?
9. What does he ask the old white man to do for him?
10. At the end of the story, who has the bottle?
11. What happens then?

IRREGULAR VERBS

be, was/ *pl* were, been
bear, bore, borne
become, became, become
begin, began, begun
blow, blew, blown
break, broke, broken
build, built, built
buy, bought, bought
can, could, (been able to)
catch, caught, caught
come, came, come
cost, cost, cost
cut, cut, cut
dig, dug, dug
do, did, done
draw, drew, drawn
drink, drank, drunk
drive, drove, driven
eat, ate, eaten
fall, fell, fallen
feel, felt, felt
fight, fought, fought
find, found, found
fly, flew, flown
forget, forgot, forgotten
get, got, got
give, gave, given
go, went, gone
grow, grew, grown
hang, hung, hung
have, had, had
hear, heard, heard
hit, hit, hit
hold, held, held
keep, kept, kept
lay, laid, laid
lead, led, led
learn, learnt/learned, learnt/learned
leave, left, left
let, let, let
lie, lay, lain

light, lit/lighted, lit/lighted
lose, lost, lost
make, made, made
may, might, (been allowed to)
mean, meant, meant
meet, met, met
must, must, (had to)
pay, paid, paid
put, put, put
read, read, read
ride, rode, ridden
ring, rang, rung
rise, rose, risen
run, ran, run
say, said, said
see, saw, seen
sell, sold, sold
send, sent, sent
set, set, set
shake, shook, shaken
shall, should, (been obliged to)
shoe, shod, shod
show, showed, shown
sing, sang, sung
sit, sat, sat
sleep, slept, slept
speak, spoke, spoken
spend, spent, spent
stand, stood, stood
strike, struck, struck
swim, swam, swum
take, took, taken
teach, taught, taught
tell, told, told
think, thought, thought
throw, threw, thrown
wear, wore, worn
will, would, (wanted to)
win, won, won
wind, wound, wound
write, wrote, written